P9-DVB-632

"When you write, must you write everything?
When you paint, must you paint everything?
All I ask is that you leave something
to my imagination..."

DIDEROT

For Pernelle...

ÉDOUARD MANCEAU

Published in North America in 2015 by Owlkids Books Inc.

Published in France under the title *C'est l'histoire d'une histoire* in 2011 by Éditions Milan

Owlkids Books acknowledges the financial support of the Canada Council for the Arts, the Ontario Arts Council, the Government of Canada through the Canada Book Fund (CBF) and the Government of Ontario through the Ontario Media Development Corporation's Book Initiative for our publishing activities.

Published in Canada by
Owlkids Books Inc.
10 Lower Spadina Avenue
Toronto, ON M5V 2Z2

Published in the United States by
Owlkids Books Inc.
1700 Fourth Street
Berkeley, CA 94710

Library and Archives Canada Cataloguing in Publication

Manceau, Édouard, 1969-
[C'est l'histoire d'une histoire English]
Once upon a rainy day / written and illustrated by Édouard Manceau ; translated by Susan Ouriou and Christelle Morelli.

Translation of: C'est l'histoire d'une histoire.
ISBN 978-1-77147-151-0 (bound)

I. Ouriou, Susan, translator II. Morelli, Christelle, translator III. Title. IV. Title: C'est l'histoire d'une histoire. English.

PZ7.M333On 2015 j843'.92 C2014-908274-6

Library of Congress Control Number: 2014958760

The text is set in ITC Avant Garde Gothic.

Manufactured in Shenzhen, Guangdong, China, in March 2015, by WKT Co. Ltd.
Job #14CB3453

A B C D E F

Édouard Manceau

Translated by Christelle Morelli and Susan Ouriou

Once Upon a Rainy Day

Owlkids Books

This is the story of a story that starts over every day, each morning the same way.

Mr. Warbler, the keeper of this story, is about to step outside his cottage in his fine feathered suit. Just as the sun rises, he will head slowly and surely down the blue path leading to the forest…

…the same path that leads straight to the home of the Big Bad Wolf, a black, hairy half-monster with pointed ears, long teeth, a cold wet nose, and a lolling tongue.

Every morning, Mr. Warbler wakes up the Big Bad Wolf with ten quick raps and three long knocks on his heavy wooden door. That's when the Big Bad Wolf appears, and his day can begin.

But today it's raining. So Mr. Warbler doesn't venture outside,
and the Big Bad Wolf sleeps in.

And so it goes. The same old story, day in, day out, except when it rains. The trees know the story well: every morning they see the Big Bad Wolf race over to Oscar's house.

Oscar is a delectable pig with plump thighs and tender feet, who takes care to keep his snout clean.

He lived in the city before moving here with his entire library. Oscar adores rainy days like today. Snuggled all cozy and warm under a tartan blanket, he devours stacks of books.

But on sunny days, it's always the same story. The Big Bad Wolf races over to catch him.

Fortunately, Oscar is a very cunning pig!

While the Big Bad Wolf tries to break down his door, Oscar escapes through a back window and jumps onto his bicycle. He pedals fast as can be over to his friend Amadeus's house to hide. The Big Bad Wolf gallops after him, yelling the same thing every time: "Blasted pig! If I catch you, I'll eat you."

Oscar always gets there first. He hides his bicycle in the bushes and slips into his friend's house.

Amadeus is a famous hare, a very clever one, who knows the woods inside out. He has lived here from the day he was born. He stores a giant stash of carrots in his little hut and, in the big hut where he sleeps, he hides a well-kept secret…

...an underground passage! Oscar and Amadeus make their way beneath the rocks to the home of their friend Niles.

Aboveground, the Big Bad Wolf howls in rage,
“Rotten hare, blasted pig! If I grab you, I’ll gut you!”

But the Big Bad Wolf never does manage to grab them as they pop out of the tunnel. Oscar and Amadeus always make it to Niles's place before him.

Niles is a flying squirrel. He traveled the world before landing in this tree one fine spring day and retiring his adventurer's gear.

In the treetop, he has built a platform for his hot-air balloon. The minute the Big Bad Wolf charges into sight, Niles grabs his little traveling trunk, helps his two friends on board, and fires up the balloon. He sets his course for the house belonging to their pal Popof, the big-mouthed bear.

The Big Bad Wolf chases after them below, throwing stones and bellowing, “Wretched squirrel, rotten hare, blasted pig! If I knock you down, I’ll gobble you up!”

But the hot-air balloon looks magnificent in the clear blue sky, soaring proudly beyond reach.

Niles grabs his telescope from his little trunk and soon spots Popof's house and Popof himself, pointing to his rooftop.

For many years, Popof was a circus clown. One summer night, he stopped here to perform with his troupe under the big top. But early the next morning when the circus left, he stayed behind to devote himself to his music.

He is very fond of Oscar, Niles, and Amadeus. When the balloon lands, Popof welcomes them with a toothy grin.

So it's always the same old story. The Big Bad Wolf shows up, and Oscar opens the door, exclaiming, "Do come in, dear friend!" The minute he's inside, Niles trips him, and Amadeus shoves him into the pipe that leads into the huge trumpet. Popof blows so hard with his enormous mouth that the Big Bad Wolf flies through the air...

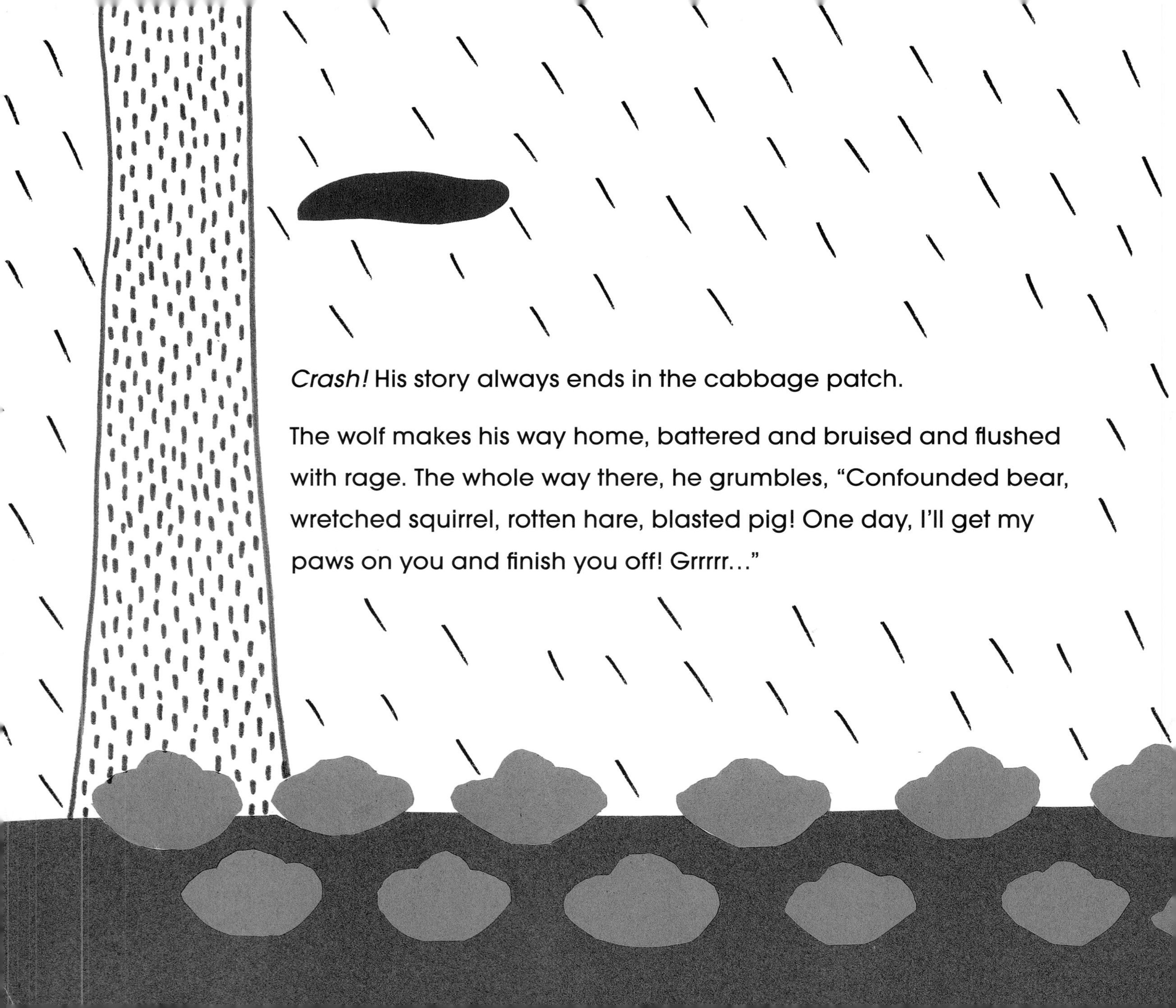

Crash! His story always ends in the cabbage patch.

The wolf makes his way home, battered and bruised and flushed with rage. The whole way there, he grumbles, “Confounded bear, wretched squirrel, rotten hare, blasted pig! One day, I’ll get my paws on you and finish you off! Grrrrr…”

But that day has yet to come, and every night the four friends celebrate at Popof's house. Together they sing:

First he tried to catch us,
Then he swore he'd gut us,
Next he vowed to gobble us up.
But he couldn't pull it off!
Now he's in the cabbage patch…
The wolf has met his match!

The next day, if the weather allows, the story begins all over again…

Actually, the rain has stopped now.

The sun is out.

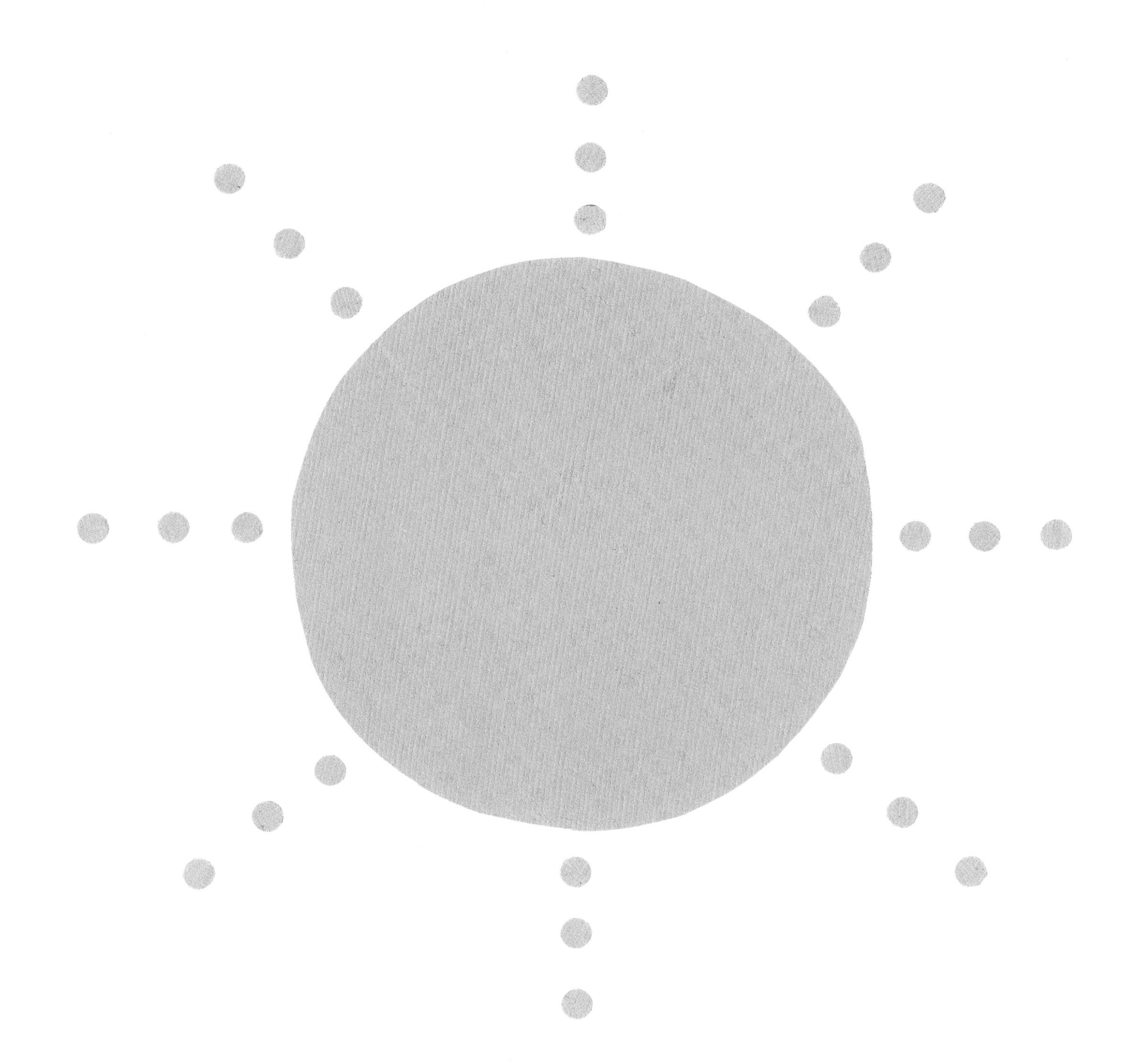

Mr. Warbler has left to wake up the Big Bad Wolf.

This time, the story can start for real...